With Yo

Every day unfolds like a thick rose,
swirls of orange-red
torrid
like your touch.
When the slow-moving clouds
creep toward the horizon
I envision you and me
somewhere in a dream,
the moments intimate
lying with you
our fingers laced
love unleashed
in red-orange bursts
lifting me
to paradise.

LOOKING FOR NAIAD?

Unstrung Heart

BY
ROBBI SOMMERS

THE NAIAD PRESS, INC.
1999

Printed in the United States of America on acid-free paper
First Edition

Editor: Christine Cassidy
Cover designer: Bonnie Liss (Phoenix Graphics)
Typesetter: Sandi Stancil

Library of Congress Cataloging-in-Publication Data

Sommers, Robbi, 1950 –
    Unstrung heart / by Robbi Sommers.
        p.   cm.
    ISBN 1-56280-239-9   (alk. paper)
    I. Title.
PS3569.O65335U55   1999
813'.54—dc21   98-46298
                                                                          CIP

Dedicated to my sons:

Justin Sommers
Nick Funk
Brian Funk

As I was saying:

Deepest love to Kate Alfieri.
She held me together before I left on my dark journey
and was there when I returned.

Special thank you to all who were there for me:

Vera Lewis
Jerry Lewis
Ellen Lewis
Michael Lewis
Marc Lewis
Anita Sachs
Selma Marcus
Kate Alfieri
Nick Funk
Brian Funk
Marty Coreia
Kate Conroy
Chesley Springer
Jonathan Marmelzat
Karen Levine
Lori Gottlieb
Dave Diamond
Peter Bodrog
Rebecca Geller
Joe Alfieri
Barbara Alfieri
Jean Maltby
Sue Brown
Michael Whitson

Once I danced barefoot
before the hornet stung
Spirit's broken
soul's unraveled
heart's unstrung.

Lost Love

Skin Hunger

Skin hunger
I'm burning
thinking of the rush
of hot summer breezes
across my breasts.
Lying in a mustard field
of sun-soaked blooms,
it's hard to see anything but the blur.
You and me
skin warm
damp
everything
yellow.
Bees shoot like darts,
ladybugs whisper
somewhere above.
I'm hungry for you —

so close
yet untouchable.
A drop of sweat
from your face
caresses my cheek.
Unbearable
this thirst for you . . .
and for those days
when I was forgiving
and uncertain
about life.
Zipping on honeybee wings
nectar so sweet
you above me
your shadow on my face.
Cool for a moment until you move
and the sun takes your place.

Spring

Spring slips into her ruffled skirts
draws me to her gauzy ways
talks me sweet and I succumb
open that first stubborn button.

She's left me breathless —
wanting to fall into a feather bed,
float down a warm stream
with you between my legs.
I'm circling like the greedy hawk
with dips and swoops on the could-be-crisp breeze.
One more button, I unhook
hoping you'll come after me,
slow dance under the old oak tree.
Spring's made a temptress out of me.

I'm standing in paradise
mesmerized.
Ardent sun
kisses —
reminds me of your lips,
warm and demanding
between my breasts.
Winter never felt this good
except that time by the fire
when we were on the floor
sticky sweet
you and me
and everything we shouldn't eat —
chocolate
and cinnamon crunch
and oh, yes, creamy cheesecake —
on my fingers.
Champagne pops between us.
You carried wood up to the room
while I sat on the bed in satin, thinking how nice
   it is
to be your girl
laughing . . .
Fire snaps and champagne bubbles
inside hazy golden moans,
your fingers
dipped in cheesecake.

Today I debate climbing a slanted ray
to the goose-down sky.
Grab your hand,
whisper in your ear,
"Honey, honey, let's go, honey."

You and I
satchel filled with fantasies
heading up
where yesterday's rainbow surprised the sky.

Spring
curtsies gracefully;
libertine dragonflies unfold their wings.
A potpourri of cellophane dreams
lift into the raised-skirt breeze
to float with sparrows between the trees.

With You

Every day unfolds like a thick rose,
swirls of orange-red
torrid
like your touch.
When the slow-moving clouds
creep toward the horizon
I envision you and me
somewhere in a dream,
the moments intimate
lying with you
our fingers laced
love unleashed
in red-orange bursts
lifting me
to paradise.

Walking on a Spring Day

Flowers break into bloom,
the air fills with lilac and rose
and God, I feel so alive —
Your hand on my belly.
Your lips on the curve of my breast.
I'll never forget.
Never.
Not one kiss, one touch, one sigh —
Nothing forgotten.
I'm walking down a street, my arms swinging,
thinking about you on a dance floor
in a smoky-blue nightclub.
Between the flash of silvery lights, you.
In the mirror, you.
In a swirling circle, you.
Across the street and up the block,
you, you, you.

The sun spills a thick heat —
you.
The sky blue and swollen —
you.
Ahead, around each corner, in every alcove.
You are the sweet spring breeze and I'm soaring
like a solitary leaf
and around — every thought
is you.
Those hot summer days . . .
In a fire-orange poppy field, you loved me.
On a deserted country road, you loved me.
Drinking tequila under a tree,
you loved me.
Always remember, you said.
And I do.
Your rough kiss in the middle of a fight,
chunks of cheese eaten without slicing,
sterling-silver roses left at my door,
Your pinky ring, that I once wore —
initialed *JT.*

I'm walking through a fragrant dream,
lost in the sensation of you
and what love was.
Those days at the ocean
hot sand squished between our toes
we were breathless —
I feel it still.
Burning —
I feel it.
I'm walking, dancing, spinning down a street
inhaling lilac and roses

thinking of you
only you
and how you loved me.
I remember your hand in mine,
kisses that sizzled,
love that promised never to die.
Around every corner, in every breath,
you.
Now, somehow, we're centuries apart,
light-years apart,
a hundred dreamless nights apart,
a thousand fading stars apart.
I walk down a street with my hands to my heart.
Not so alive — not anymore.
The sun has slithered behind a cloud.
The scent of wildflowers has crumbled and died.
The chill in the air promises to stay
and the wind lifts a memory
to usher her away.

Four Packs of Sugar

You walked into the café
smiled
avoided the chair across from me
didn't put the small, round table between us
but stepped close — your hand on mine
your lips against my cheek.

You knew.
Without a word, you knew.
You could read my eyes.
I steadied myself. Looked the other way.
You could feel my desire. Always could. Always would.
And you're so clever. You can hypnotize, make me
desert every promise I've ever made.
I will see you, I'd said. **But I won't
want you. I won't want**

you. I won't want you.
Your hand rested on mine,
your lips, soft on my cheek —
"Good to see you," you said.
My slight nod
a meek reply.
I was tied up
concentrating
trying to hold my ground.
Even so, against my will,
I remembered
that day at the coast.
We sat on a cliff overlooking the sea
drank wine right out of the bottle
tore bread from a just-baked loaf
ate fresh crab with our fingers . . .

My eyes burned.
You were so close,
your mouth on my cheek,
your hand on mine.
You were thinking about the ocean, it was in
    your eyes.
Your mouth
so close
to mine
I could barely suppress the urge to kiss you.
What had I been thinking? Meeting you like this.
This was your way
to trick me out of myself and into you.
All my promises
in a lazy spin.

I'd seen it all before.
A hypnotist, that's what you are.

Your hand lifted from mine and you sat in the chair
across the round table
so far from me.
I wanted you. Wanted you. Wanted you.
Was that so wrong?
My heart raced
my eyes stung
and somewhere, far away,
broken promises coiled into the summer sky.
"How have you been," is what you said.
You miss me, is what you meant.
I knew it and so did you. That's the way it was
between us.
"Really great," I said, my mouth dry,
the dryness in my eyes too harsh.
"Still so in love?" You squeezed my hand
and headed for the counter.
Still so in love. You were clever that way.
Saying one thing, meaning another.
Still so in love with my new lover,
was what you'd implied.
Still so in love with you, is what you'd meant.
"Yes," I called to you,
too loud. Too obvious. "I couldn't be happier."
You sat back down. Cup of coffee and a smile. Stirred
in four packs of sugar —
you liked it sweet.
You nodded. Smiled. Touched my hand. "Nice day,
 huh."
I glanced out the window. Sun high. Sky blue.

"I got business out at the coast. Wanna come along
for the ride?"

Hands dipped in soft crab bellies
the fruity wine flows free, and between us,
one perfect daffodil bouquet.

Tart

Tart
like that first night you slept with me
and I gave way to your magic charms.
Snakes slithered somewhere across the room.
I didn't care,
didn't see them,
then,
when your kiss blinded me
and those glamorous words you wore
decorated all the dirty secrets
you kept under wraps.
Tart
like the crisp night air
deep in my chest
as I gasped,
called your name,
the pleasure

deafening.
Couldn't hear the rattle of the tails
warning me
beware
snakes all over the floor.

One Lone Rose

I fill the tub
slowly step in
too hot doesn't ease this tension
torturous
long minutes
until your call.

Rhinestones beaded, strung on lamps.
Lilac-scented sheets turned down.
I'm waiting
this eternity
without you.
Telephone by the tub
I'm enslaved.
Not like it used to be
when I was the one
who made the calls

those days
before you.

I wait
sinking like rose quartz
underwater.
All's quiet
except the sound of bubbles bursting.

Are you in your garden?
One lone rose
blooming,
fresh-picked,
its floral spice
spinning scents.
Do you remember my perfume?
One thorn,
smooth yet sharp
against your thumb.
A drop of blood
smears white petals
as I sink beneath the bubbles,
their snaps against my skin.

Candle spills
its liquid flame
between my breasts,
burns like your kiss
Beneath bubbles
the crimson wax sizzles.

Towel rough,
scraped dry

I wait
lipstick red
on my lips.
Fingertips
brush across my linen dress.
I wait
for your call.

Petals wilt before too long.
Streaked in red
dressed in white
I count the minutes —
fifty-one, fifty-two.
Watch the phone.
Wait for you.

Are you in your garden
with determined pace
a cocksure smile upon your face?

Stare at the phone,
wait for you.
Fifty-nine, sixty,
sixty-one, sixty-two.

I Know Her

Black night
moon rides the once-studded sky doomed and broken.
Knitted shadows barely creep.
I know the meaning of regret —
her bruises on my back.
Shoulders slumped, I walk
no longer restless
too accustomed
to the weight.
Anyway
I know about her —
regret.
Voices, thin and shaken.
Severed hearts still strain to connect
invisible abyss too wide for one last touch?
we wonder
wearing disbelief like mourners' veils.

Locked

Would you like to meet me
in the mist of a dream,
on the flat of a rock,
near the bank of a stream?
I'd weave camouflaged love
between strands of wild clover —
twist flower to stem,
knot stem to white flower.
A stretched floral braid
I'm sure could close this distance.

In a dream you saw us
sitting on a rock —
we talked about open doors,
flashed keys for rusted locks.

Say that you'll dream us there.
Tell me that it's *yes*.
I'll tie purple ribbons in my hair,
wear that breezy, yellow dress.

Close your eyes. Dream us.
You at least owe me that.
You promised we would always have
that rock
where we sat.

Circles

I turn in slow circles.
A broken moon casts pinpoints of light
across the charred sky.
It's difficult to decipher
what the darkness holds.
Long ago, you convinced me —
stars were diamonds sewn by Eros.
You whispered secrets
of draped darkness.
An ingénue, I believed your promises.

Tonight,
that same canopy of glitter revolves above me.
Diamonds on velvet, you'd said.
No longer a romantic —
I understand the provocative weaving

of hope and lies.
A venomous spider spins silk temptation.

Eros's diamonds sewn to the sky.
Another lie.
It was Eros —
oh yes, that much was true.
Drunk and alone,
he hurled a stray barb,
spearing the quixotic moon.
Shattered and broken,
pebbles of light
scattered across the sky.

A woman stared at the sky,
awaiting Eros's elixir —
unaware that the love-dipped lance
meant for her
was flung by Eros on a binge,
caught in a careless wind,
lifted far from a waiting heart,
flew off course,
and harpooned the moon.

I move in lazy circles.
A crash had roused me from sleep.
I ripped the covers aside
hurried to the window
just in time
to see the full moon crack.
Stones of light were strewn across the sky.

I raced down the stairs,
out the door
into the night.
Could I —
if I raised my arms high enough,
opened my palms wide enough —
capture the drizzling light?

Had anyone else seen it?
Somewhere, I was certain
another love-torn woman stood in her yard —
her hands open to the sky —
hoping to catch a palmful of light.

Crumpled on a door stoop,
Eros grasped his empty bottle
and begged for spare change.
Eventually, he'd gamble the last of his arrows
for the chance
of a momentary high . . .
And what then?
What about us?
The ones who saw?

The sky revolves above me.
With each completed circle,
the twinkling light
sinks deeper into darkness.
Is the sky moving farther from me
or am I simply drifting away?
I slow to a standstill
then sink to the cool grass.

Eros slumps in a deserted doorway
and somewhere far away,
the chance for love crumbles.

Lunar Eclipse

Against my will
I sit on the back porch and stare at the night sky.
I don't want to be here.
I wish I could escape.
Too late
I'm a victim of your sorcery.
An eclipse is just
another excuse to cast a spell,
another way to lure me into the dark.
Your magic unrolls from the sky like a black net.
I search for the first star.
I wish I may, I wish I might,
escape this web you've spun tonight.
Filigree memories capture me.
The midnight sky
spills like satiny ink —
Drenched with you, I cross the dew-dampened lawn,

stuff my hands in my pockets
and push through the tightly meshed night.
Your magic, a black veil.
Isn't it enough that you've disappeared
in a puff of thin smoke
abracadabra
my heart slipped up your silky sleeve?

Ruby Dream

Covered with red sequins —
like rubies
struck by lightning,
electric shoes on fire —
showcased in the window
of a glitzy shop on Main.

Perhaps it was the urge
to flirt with transformation?
Perhaps it was a moon
suspended in Leo?
I'll never know for certain
how unconscious motivations
seized control.

An unadorned girl,
neglected,

blossoms insecurities.
Ask Cinderella's benefactor
why she waved her wand.

What would it take
to waltz with a stranger
before the clock strikes twelve?
Could *I* leave a prince still yearning,
my lost slipper in his hand?

The night before I bought them
I dreamed I wore the shoes:
I was me . . . yet I had splintered
into ruby lights that glimmered
on mirrored walls surrounding
a dreamy ballroom floor.

I Know This

Vulnerable candle
blue flame meets black
wax weeps like teardrops ...
slow,
continual.
I know this.
Memories streak my pillow
melted, then hardened.
I know this.
Stare and wonder
those smoky lost dreams
twisted thin streams
hazy
hypnotic
surprisingly unknotted and free —
they court a blank moon
a scarred sky

with choked flame.
I know this
drowning
shamed
flickering pain.
Liquid yesterdays blurred and dripping.
Smeary, weak and too soon petrified
once-tall candle
vanishing.

Splinters

If I crouched in a corner
and tucked into myself
could I believe
I'm just a child —
and nightmares are dreams
that evaporate
with the flip of a light switch?
I mean,
if that's the truth
that someone comes,
I would.

If I could run down a glorious hill
spin with glee over buttercups
leap over jagged rocks
and broken glass
that just sparkles,

I would . . .
I mean
if scrapes were easily kissed away —
if that's the truth
I would.

If I could disappear,
while someone counts to fifty —
and end up safe behind a tree.
If there's such a place
and it was true
that hide-and-seek was just a game
and when we're done, we come in free —
I would.

If I could return to fairy tales
where once upon a time
meant *happily ever after*
and I fell asleep
with a child's smile?
I mean . . .
if that's the truth,
I would.

If I concentrate?
If I meditate?
If I stared into the light
closed my eyes
would it still be bright?
Could I slice darkness
and revive each thin color,
concealed and murky?
I mean,

if darkness was simply a rainbow
run amok
coagulated
melted from too much heat.
If that's the truth
and I could splinter
every hue,
I would.

Wings

Eros met me in the airport restaurant
on an early Sunday morning.
He'd smuggled in two cinnamon buns
beneath a worn bomber jacket.
A special treat, is what he said,
and after,
licked the sticky sweet
from my fingers.
I felt sugary anyway —
that's how Eros does love.

He walked me to the Piper Cub
he'd rented for the day.
He wanted me to fly with him
to close my eyes
and just step in.
I shook my head.

There was no way
I'd go up in that plane.
I promise I'd wait for him,
surefooted on the ground.

As though he hadn't heard a word,
he reached into the plane.
He then revealed a golden pouch
opened it
and pulled out
a pair of wings
fluffy white
and fragrant as white clover.

Eros has his clever tricks.
He changes minds
He's very slick.
I mean, I *think* that's what I saw —
fluffy wings, three feet tall.
Eros made me want to believe —
that's what he does best.

"This is how we'll fly," he said.
His eyes held crimson fire.
He clipped the wings
onto his shoulders,
pulled me close
as the wings fluttered.
He kissed me tender on my lips —
that's how Eros flies.

Charade

Once I learned to shape-shift
with the wave of a wand,
I could disappear
and reappear
with one quick breath.
I removed the tight cocoon
woven by love's pain
and slipped into another form —
Ruby
couldn't be touched,
and felt no pain,
once I waved the wand.

A fresh bouquet
has no choice
but to wilt and slowly fade.
Silk petals were a sweet disguise.

They tricked the eyes
with their charade ...
once I waved the wand.

Ruby ran with Eros.
She'd met him on the street.
He taught her to see in the dark
aim an arrow,
hit her mark,
slip through fingers,
tempt
intrigue
up the ante
tease,
deceive ...
play the odds,
shoot the dice,
flirt with power,
vamp
entice.

Once I learned to wave the wand
I disappeared.

Birds of Prey

I lie in bed next to you.
The blue light of insomnia snaps and sparks.
I'm weary
of this battle.

You sleep —
so peaceful, that life of yours,
unsuspecting of the vultures circling overhead . . .
The remains of past lovers are invisible
skeletons scattered across my floor.
They slept soundly, too.
Once, when I loved them.

Making love with you,
is honeyed escape
thick and full.
But beyond gray clouds that you can't see

high above the reflected blue
of silver-lined love,
ravenous predators
float like songbirds —
it's a matter of perspective
what you see
when you look at the sky.

The flesh-eaters seem to follow me
and all over the floor
bones are picked clean.

The Dove and Fall of Night

At the foot of the mountain, a lone dove rests.
Hypnotized, she stares toward the horizon.
The red sun melts, streaking the sky
with the blood of oncoming night.

The dove shivers then huddles into herself.
A passerby would surely dismiss her
as a mound of unpacked snow.
Just as well.
Isn't she all that's left of the avalanche?
Wasn't there, not long ago,
a devastating storm?

Behind a not-too-distant tree, I hid.
Ran for cover, that's what I did.

That's what we all did
except the dove entangled in spiked crystal flakes.

Blood drips from the despair of day and stains us all.
I have bruises . . .
Come look, I'll raise my blouse.
Purple-black still rides my belly.

And what of the dove
who refused to move?
Incapable of flight?
Too frightened?
Too brave?
She shivers in a frozen ball.

And me?
I'm behind a tree
watching the dove
as the sky goes black.

Convertible

I dreamed about you last night.
It was a rendezvous.
Were we at our best?
Hard to remember anymore,
our best.
That dream —
you and I
cruising back roads
in your silver Porsche
top down,
always —
you liked desire
windblown and dazzled.
Cruising
fast and smooth,
down double yellow lines
breaking rules

all the way.
You liked it reckless
and with you,
so did I.

We were waking from the nightmare
of all those long, long days apart.
To see you again, in a dream!
We were so free —

I had that feeling;
remember when?
The speed climbed
and I got scared.
"Don't worry," you said. "I've got you."
Your fingers woven in mine.
Secure
with you at the wheel.
We were racing time,
rode shooting stars,
at least that's what you said.
A dream —
the fertile sky ached,
overripe with stars.
The swollen moon threatened to spill.
"Let's drink the light," you said,
and passed me a crystal goblet.

The eclipse
left a shadow across your face.
I wore sunglasses
while your smile hid the darkness in your eyes.

I suspect you peeked when you took a sip.
Temptation was your weakness.

I awoke
intoxicated . . .
immersed in you
drowning in you,
the absolute pain of missing you
chiseled in my breast.
As the room spun
I wondered
if you had opened your eyes
and discovered
you'd been blinded.

Royal Flush

Ruby awoke and reached for her mask
knocked over the oil lamp, the now empty flask.
The crash to the floor hurled me out of my dreams
and into the middle of her crazy schemes.

"I was *something* last night," Ruby said with a grin.
"Played poker with Eros after six shots of gin."
"Eros?" I mumbled and glanced at the floor.
Oil from the lamp slowly oozed toward the door.

"The window is open, that's dangerous," I said,
thinking, *Why must she always bring risk to my bed*?
"Danger?" she answered and smiled in her way.
"A royal flush — hearts — a remarkable play."

Eros came through the window — he likes to intrigue
Of course, *you* were sleeping — you're not in *our*
  league.
He brought fiery arrows that he uses for love —
With shafts of fine gold and a feathery dove."

"He *also* has arrows that are leaden and foul
with feathers he's plucked from the breast of an
  owl."
I hoped she was listening. Sometimes she didn't care
for opinions and facts that I often would share.

I'd read all about it in legends and myths:
the owl brings indifference — that was *his* gift.
I crossed my arms — my point being clear.
It's not hate that I dreaded, but indifference I feared.

"The owl? Not to worry." Ruby put on her mask.
She reached for the whiskey and filled up her flask.
"Owl feathers, lead arrows, are simple illusions
for lovers entrenched in romantic delusions."

Her laugh was cocky as she climbed from the bed.
I don't think she noticed that arrow of lead.
Her bare foot fell victim, the slice seemed severe...
She kept on walking — was she *that* unaware?

A thin trail of blood followed her to the door.
"Suppose I'll find love now?" She laughed all the
  more.
"Owl feathers," I stammered, "won't bring love at
  all!"
Did she not realize the owl brings a fall?

Ruby glared through eyes that were cut in her mask.
"Why must you make everything such a task?
Indifference is simply a way to achieve
the sort of love that fascinates me."

She pulled on her jeans, put on a green sweater.
She looked just like me, only many times better.
She'd go shopping — *I knew it* — for someone to lure
while I wipe the blood and oil from the floor.

Fast Cars

I walk down a back road,
lost in another dream.
Hung from my shoulder
a golden pouch holds
tarnished shoes,
half-plucked wings
and an impotent magic wand.

A silver Porsche slows next to me —
for a moment
I think
that it's JT,
but the top is up,
the windows too —
not JT's style.

The window unwinds slowly.
Inside the driver smiles.
I point beyond the yellow lines
that once led lovers to the sky.
"Can you get me there?" is all I say.
"Get in," is her reply.

I lay the pouch between us,
certain the ride is long.
Passing fields are orange streaks
as I drift into slumber.

My golden pouch lays empty
when I open my eyes.
The driver's mouth curls to a smirk.
Her dark words cut the silence.
"They're gone, I sold them miles ago.
Not every ride is free."

"Pull over!" I cry, but the car doesn't slow.
I open the door
and leap.
A sea of poppies captures me.
A crow descends into a tree.
The continual hum
of cars whizzing by
beckons me.

Suddenly,
I see them pass —
convertible down,
going fast.
In the Porsche,

Ruby drives
while Eros holds his bow up high.
They look as though they'll reach the sky
on double yellow lines.

Blessed Be

She sends me razor-edged notes
I can barely see half the time anyway blood smeared
   and
everything soaked
in it
Rusted dry pain
caked
Cracked lines crisscross —
my breast holds a map to hell (and back — I'd like
   to say)
I don't blame her most of the time
stiletto words line my heart too
those dark nights and dismal days
when anger and hurt crowd the room.
I whisper only to mirrors
invisible-ink murmurs show themselves then stray
Blessed Be

I'm trying
to walk in God
whatever that means
forgive and be forgiven.

Love's many faces.
I open the letters she sends
sometimes soft
sometimes jagged
prism-in-a-window words reflect
teeny rainbows circle the room
or a dead bird drops from a stark black tree
outside trapped in winter's misery.
She's tightened
into a ball,
like me.
Honed words
slit wrists
walk in God
Blessed Be.

Child, Lost

Missing Justin

I wake up struck by that first horrid second of the
  new day.
Immediately, the loss of you conquers me.
Engulfed with grief, I lie in bed and stare at the
  thin streak of light between the blinds.
Another day
without you.
Hollow grief spirals, slowly knotting into a black
  stone.
Devastating pain
pummels me like a storm of burning hail.
Bruised and weakened, I climb from bed
and stumble through an empty house —
looking for you.
Hurry out the door into a gray-draped morning —
frantic for you.
Into the tear-stained dawn

where death's chill wraps me like a mourner's
   shroud,
I'm searching for a sign.
Perhaps a silver streak blazing across the sky?
You see, Mom, here I am, fiery and alive.
I'm not gone. See me! Up here!
A platinum arc soaring like a shooting star —
See, Mom, here!
Desperate, I scan the sky.
Justin?
Justin?
A rainbow-driven sunrise slowly unveils.
Dear Justin, is that you?
Spilling pinks and golds across the lifeless sky?
A leaf swirls from a tree in an emerald pirouette.
Justin, is that you?
A feather on cement?
A four-leaf clover in a field of green?
A heads-up penny under a bush?
Justin, tell me, is that you
assuring me
that you're okay?
Every step I take, I search
for you,
some sign
of you,
some way to know.
Justin, sweet, loved Justin,
I'm desperate to find my way to you.
The loss slithers in my throat
strangles me
squeezes the life from me.
A spiral of black butterflies

weaves a mournful tapestry across the sky.
I wander in a daze,
confused and uncertain —
a bitter ache coiled in my belly like an angry snake.
Each heartbeat pumps cruel venom
a stinging poison.
Every cell of my being cries, screams, wails,
soaked with the excruciating pain
of losing
you
Justin.
Sweet Justin.
Where are you?
Death's jagged blade has carved your name in
    my flesh.
My grief
seeps like blood from an uneven wound.
Justin, Justin, Justin.
I will keep searching,
never stopping,
every step
always looking —
in the morning sky, I will find you.
In a blooming rose, I will find you.
A spring breeze,
a drop of summer rain,
I promise, my sweet Justin
I will find you.
There and there and everywhere
Every single breath
Every blink of the eye
Every laugh
Every tear

Every cloud
Every butterfly
My son, my friend, my darling boy
I'll search the sky for a silver streak of stars
And find you there
I promise.

An Unmarked Grave

I tear petals from the flowers
and watch them fall
across the still-rounded sod of an unmarked grave.
Somewhere, down there,
somewhere
beneath my feet,
he lies
and I stand helpless,
unable to hold him
unable to wipe the tears from his eyes,
a mother's nightmare . . .
My child needs me
and
and
and
there's nothing I can do,

nothing . . .
I want to dig through the dirt with
my fingers,
my teeth —
uncover him
hold him.
I scream at the trees
beg the sky,
Bring him back!
What will it take
to undo this mistake?
My heart torn from my chest?
Already done.
My belly sliced?
Done. Done. Done.
What will it take?

I kissed him that last day,
pale flesh against my lips.
Death, blue and empty, flowing up
his fingers in a deadly stream.
I whispered his name
called his name
cried his name.
No answer.
No answer still.
Cold flesh against a mother's lips,
how could this be?
Someone make this stop,
wind back time,
make it go away . . .
Death, cold and blue, seeps under locked doors,

through double-paned glass.
Every breath I take, cold and empty.

Helpless, I stare at the fresh-mowed grass
my mouth, still locked in a silent scream,
today and forever.
And petals spill from flowers,
leaving a blurred trail of wilted colors
on an unmarked grave.

Disappearing

I stand on the bank and peer into the river:
a leaf twirls
a water spider glides.
My reflection thins by the second.
An indistinct blur
wavering
on a passing stream
disappearing
into nothing.

Nothing

I say absolutely nothing.
She sits across from me, silent.
I peer at my watch.
Ninety-five an hour . . .
I could be home, ninety-five dollars richer.
"I sense that you're angry." She breaks the silence.
Who cares? A waste of time, that's what this is.
I shrug.
"I'm not angry," I mutter.
She nods.
I glance around the room.
No, not angry.
My son is dead . . .
devastated, yes.
heartbroken, yes.
Stunned, ruined,
yes, yes, yes.

But angry?
Angry?
My jaw suddenly aches — I'm clenching again.
Angry?
No.
With nothing to say, I close my eyes . . .
I see myself pacing
back and forth beside his grave,
nothing to say . . .
Back and forth, a predatory horror trails behind me,
each step
back and forth
lunging at my heels.
Angry?
No, not angry.
Somewhere —
from the trees? —
a sniper aims.
A bullet, tipped with death's despair,
rips through my chest.
I stumble to the ground,
gasping for air.
I bury my face in the grass-covered grave . . .
Angry?
How can I feel anger?
How can I feel anything but the relentless need
to somehow climb into that grave
and wake him up?
Lie underneath him and
push,
push,
push
the breath out of me,

into him.
My eyes burn with the pain of missing him.
My body aches as if I've been twisted inside out.
I carry a lead weight in my chest,
in my belly.
I am raw
and wounded and bleeding and it just doesn't stop . . .
Lie underneath him and
blow,
blow,
blow
the breath out of me,
into him.
Wake him,
push him,
as I did twenty-one years before,
from a womb of darkness into the light where he
    belongs.
Underneath him, and
push,
push,
push . . .

"Where did you just go?" Her words pull me back.
I shrug again. "I went
to the cemetery this morning — I was
thinking about that."
"And?"
Jesus. What difference does it make?
None.
She knows that. I know that.
There's nothing either of us can do.
Pointless.

I glance at my watch.
Ten more minutes. One dollar and ninety cents per
    minute.
I reach for my purse. "I've got nothing more to say."
She is silent.
"So, I'm going to go . . ."
Silence still.
I look her straight in the eyes, stand up.
"See you next week."
She smiles and nods.

From her office, I step into the jagged sunlight.
My jaw aches.
My eyes sting.
There's no place to go.
He's dead, dead, dead.
No place to go that will make that change.
No place to go that can change that truth.
Spinning . . .
Spinning with him in my arms . . . Mommy loves you.
Mommy loves you forever and ever.
Laughing
Mommy loves you,
Mommy loves you.
The breeze slices at my skin.
Everywhere razor-sharp pain lashes at me.
Mommy loves you
Mommy loves you
Push,
push,
push him from the dark and into life's light.
I promised him, no monster in the closet,
but what about this?

What about this?
This horrible monster that swooped like a giant
    buzzard
and snatched him.
I turned away for a second?
I blinked an eye?
One minute, and he's gone?
Who could protect him from that?
"No, see, come look — no monster in the closet."
Him with a squirt gun clenched in his hand.
Who would have guessed,
the monster was behind us all along.

One Certainty

I miss Justin.
He's gone.
The rest of my life
wherever I go
whatever I do
he will never
walk through the front door,
give me a hug
kiss me hello
grinning — hat turned on his head,
too cool sunglasses concealing his eyes
never
never see him again.
The rest of my life
one certainty —
never
see

Justin
again.
It's over,
he's gone.
Never
see
him
never, ever again.
Each day melts into the next
certain of one thing —
he's gone.
Never coming home,
or laughing at my jokes
or asking for a loan
or talking about his fears.
Nope
none of that.
One certainty:
No fresh start
no bright sun filled with hope
nope, none of that . . .
Canopied by everlasting gloom,
walking with a certainty
I
can't
bear
life unwinds
a hopeless trail into the future.
With no place to turn,
I stand frozen.
Am I expected to go forward
and leave my child behind?
One certainty,

no Justin,
not ahead
wherever the path leads
certain of
one horrid truth.
No Justin.
Never
ever
again.

A Corkscrew Willow Tree

Today we planted a corkscrew willow tree.
Its promise —
to fill the sky with spiral leaves
in the garden,
our memorial
to you.
The roses offer red and yellow blooms though
it's only been two months
since we began planting...
The ground, like us,
reluctant to surrender.
The haunting sound of dirt
        falling
                into
                        a hole
too familiar.
The last time,

at your grave, that sound
again and again
as dirt tumbled onto a smooth pine box
and people sobbed
tears streamed and someone cried, "No, no, no."
Or was that me?
One by one we lifted the shovel
and shared the task of spilling dirt,
covering you, until you couldn't be seen,
delivering you back to the womb —
birth-labor once so sweet,
but O God, O God —
I gave you back against my will.
A cruel sound
thud
thud
covering the last traces of the smooth pine box
while I tossed broken-stemmed flowers after each
   shovelful
thud
thud
and someone was moaning, "No, no, no."
The sky torn and a teary mist
so cool, it blurred the sounds.
Thud, thud, thud.
Again.
Again.
Flowers flung into a grave — nothing
left to offer but inevitable wilt . . .
And what about you?
What about you
down there
under the weight of freshly turned dirt?

thud
thud
Again, again,
relentless,
cruel
and someone was screaming, "No, no, no."
Was that me?
peering into the ripped ground
that swallowed a child
with one thick gulp.
And all the while, broken flowers gasped
for one last chance . . .

Today,
butterflies twirled
like orange musical notes
and curious birds watched
my young sons
packing the dirt,
watering —
sweat on their brows
sun beating down
pollen-drunk bees
hovering
between velvet-fringed petals . . .
all awaiting
the lovely spiral promise
of a corkscrew willow tree.

If Only I Could

I stand at your grave and try not to think of a
    body,
somewhere below
continuing its slow deterioration.
The once-warm flesh
the laughing eyes
the mouth
the hair
the strong arms —
I try not to think of what must be happening
down there, beneath my feet.
High above me,
that's where you are.
Up there
behind death's veil.
I feel you, everyday, I feel you.
Somewhere,

behind the blue tears of loss
beyond death's one-way mirror
that's where you are
skiing the slopes of a soft white cloud,
sporting a new, even-cooler pair of sunglasses.
Tan and full of new-sprung life . . .
Or maybe
in a heavenly designer store
spending eternity on a shopping spree . . .
Or is it like New York City where you've gone?
And you and your new buddies
are making the scene
in a shiny sports car
so-much-cash in your wallets
Versace jackets
that smile on your face.
Oh, yes, I know your dreams . . .
At least the dreams you used to have.
I know the life you wanted, the life
you maybe would have lived . . .
I know your dreams,
at least the ones you had
when you were here.
Stopping by with a bag of new clothes
showing each thing you bought
talking about a jacket you still wanted to buy,
never enough cash
after all, that's how life is . . .
I mean, *was*.
I'd buy you anything if you'd just stop by
today —
five minutes
please?

Somehow, I'd get the cash and take you anywhere
    you wanted to go
and buy you everything
and pay off your debts
and solve all your problems
and make it okay
and throw myself in front of the car
that took you to the party
that night
you died.
Lie in front of the car,
that's what I'd do,
or go to the party and make sure you'd be okay
and sit with you, watch over you, take care of you
like a mother should,
if she could
if she could
if she could . . .
Are you somewhere, up there,
behind the thin screen
driving to Mexico?
Swimming in an ocean?
Talking to girls?
Laughing like you do? Are you?
Are you?
Because you're not in the ground,
NO. NO. NO.
Not in the ground.
Do you hear me?
No, you can't go to the party.
No!
You can't join the fraternity.
No!

You can't go to college.
You can't leave home.
No! No! No!
You will stay here. You will stay here
and I'll watch over you . . .
If only I could.
If only I could.
Instead,
I lay my bouquet
at the head of your grave
walk to the car
without looking back.

A Bottle of Bubbles
and a Hummingbird

I sit in your garden.
One breath
and a flurry of bubbles somersault in the breeze.
Tiny chimes clink from the willow tree
and a hummingbird worships an eager flower.

I used to wonder, but now, I'm certain —
Those prism-tinted bubbles that dance on the wind
disappear in a sudden burst.
And the hummingbird's once-adored blossom,
no matter how sweet,
is soon abandoned.

Seasons Change

I climb from the car.
Just yesterday, the sky was blue
but today, it's muted and gray.
The first hint of the changing season
is sudden, unexpected.
It only gets worse . . .
Bleak winter approaches.
The warmth of the sun, the cobalt sky,
were kind distractions.
Summer is withering.
Four leaves, limp and faded, lie defeated on your
    grave.
Soon, the full-leafed tree that guards you
will be bare-branched and gloomy —
nothing more than a stark silhouette to greet me as
    I make that horrid walk
down to your grave.

What's to look forward to? That's what I want to
    know.
Every day — continual deterioration . . .
It started last spring when the telephone rang
your dad's voice broken,
"I've got really bad news . . ."
My heart sinking.
My throat tight.
Desperate, I muttered, "What?"
If I had screamed "No!" and slammed down the
    phone,
would today be different?
If I had refused to answer that call,
would life be filled with hope?
Could I have somehow stopped the tidal wave of
    devastation
that poured through the doors,
the windows . . .
But no —
with phone clamped in hand, I'd cried, **"What?
    What? What?"**
Even though I knew,
deep inside,
there was nothing he could say that I'd want to
    hear —
all I could do was moan, **What?**
"Justin died this morning."
Who says those words to a mother?
Something sharp corkscrewed into my heart,
hasn't stopped.
Who says those words to a mother?
Justin
died

this
morning —
Something was draining from me —
like blood,
like spirit,
like life.
I no longer could feel myself
as I clenched the phone.
". . . this morning," he said.
"Emergency room," he said.
Who says those words to a mother?
Around me, everything started to freeze,
my life turned to ice —
never thawed,
never will.
Spring into summer into fall . . .
A stark silhouette where a tree used to be.
Time keeps passing,
but how can that be?
Minutes into days into weeks —
moving so fast . . . **how can that be?**
The relentless second hand circles the clock,
slipping further away from your last breath.
Tick, tick, tick,
you
slipping further
from me.
One crucial second,
one breath before the last.
I want to go back to then,
that last second of life,
lie down next to you,
lose consciousness for you . . .

Take the pain of CPR,
the hard rush of epinephrine,
the sharp jolt of electricity again and again —
to make you breathe or wake or come back to life,
all those desperate attempts that should have
but didn't
work . . .
Where was God then?
Where was God then?
I wasn't there,
but I can see it all —
forcing air into your mouth,
waiting for your lungs to work,
massaging your heart,
searching for that telltale beat,
one beat that separates you from me,
pounding your chest,
shocking your heart.
No mother there to scream "Justin, honey,
please come back!"
Where was God then?
Again and again,
strangers trying to jump-start your heart,
trying to pull your soul back to the blue-tinted flesh.
Where was God then,
that's what I want to know.
They pushed
and pounded
and shoved
and jolted
a heart that brought me joy —
now rebelling, refusing to start —
again and again, they worked, until someone

shook her head and closed her eyes . . .
and yours . . .
All that effort smashed to a moment of silence —
there's nothing to say
when a twenty-one-year-old boy
passes away . . .
except,
Have the parents been located?

Glimmer

The first storm —
I hate it
nonstop pounding on the window
like memories . . .
your coffin sinking into the grave
last spring,
an ordinary day . . .
I suppose flowers were blooming,
who looked?
Who could see beyond your death?
Spring had folded to a sudden close
and blue was sucked from the sky,
the air so thin that I was faint,
the reason to breathe drowned
by the silent sobs
that would not stop.

Muffled thunder shakes the midnight sky.
Last April
I screamed your name,
stiletto-pain stabbing my heart
as I lay crumpled and ruined on the floor.
Tear-stained and hoarse
I cut your name into my flesh —
an ancient rite to proclaim my grief.
But blood-red letters couldn't convey
the depth of my despair.

Tonight, a midnight storm.
A pale scar on my arm is all that remains . . .
Getting on with life — what does that mean?
Every night, I toss and turn,
my legs ache, my feet burn with pins and needles.
Is my entire body slowly going numb
or am I weak from the vitamins I've forgotten
   to take?
It's hard to know what is what
these days,
anymore,
since you died.
Crimson letters carved in skin —
J . . . U . . . S . . . T . . . I . . . N
razor in hand,
curious that there was no pain
when I sliced the word . . . not near the vein
but wondering about that too.

Lately, there are stretches of time
when everything is still —
a kind of after-storm calm.

Am I turning to stone?
Or
even worse
is this quiet the first glimmer of relief . . .
a glimpse of some future tranquility.
Healing?
I'm frightened to think —
afraid to consider
the dwindling of grief.
What then?
What would I do?
Without the despair that connects me to you,
keeping you here in some curious way
I can't explain.
Nonstop grief — my umbilical cord to you
wherever you are
my baby
floating in a womb far away.

Or maybe,
dare I hope?
I'll stay stuck in limbo — like my legs and feet —
   aching but asleep?
I don't know.
I can't tell.
I force through each day
like a reluctant dark moon.
I push myself back into life
because I should
dulled and distant
trying to seek shelter from a storm of pain
yet dreading the day that it goes away.
"You're beginning to heal."

That's what *they* pray.
But I don't know,
I can't say
if it's all right to
betray you that way.

Ritual

I hate it,
these rituals I have because you are dead.
A candle, every night,
desperate words whispered to a single flame.
Rituals
that I would never wish on any mother.
O God, and that horrid walk to the grave
spreading flower petals over you
wishing there was some way to keep you warm
as the sun drains into the dull sky.
I want to hug you but all I can do is kiss the grass.
There's nothing else,
it's the best I can do.
Summer's dying
soon the chilling rain will come.
I'll be here,
still.

No umbrella can protect you
no blanket, no coat.
You —
under there —
never warm enough.

Another season on its way,
and still, I'm helpless.
No matter what I've imagined,
I haven't devised a ritual to bring you back.
Time moves on.

While You Were Sleeping

While you were sleeping
I slipped three lilies into the vase
below the stone that has your name carved.
The dates glared at me
like some kind of monster
black and gloomy
on a ripe spring day.
Three lilies, orange and yellow,
as if, somehow, the bright colors might reflect
   the sun
and wake you from that never-ending slumber.
Someone said that time will pass and the pain will
   lessen
but I know the truth about time.
That minute, when the telephone rang
and your father's voice
shaken and broken

said those words
I've got really bad news
that minute never passed.
Instead it ballooned into a vast
empty
ongoing
deluge of pain.
I think suicide.
I think of all the ways I can find my way to you.
I'm trapped in a lifeless rolling nightmare.
It's hard to cry, let down the wall,
an avalanche will bury me...

I died too
I know that.
I died the moment I heard his voice
telling me you died
and my heart screamed,
No.

No escape from this
long
horrid
minute
that will not end.

How do I find my way to you?
Not even one year has passed — that same minute
    blown
into eternity
slow motion
slices of that moment stretched

as I got into the car and drove those three long
    hours
to the warehouse
that slum of death
where they store the bodies.
You lay on a metal slab,
covered with a sheet
one hand lifted
raised toward me?
Toward God?
Color had drained,
fingertips faded
blue.
Nothing could have prepared me —
I climbed onto the table next to you
hanging on
never wanting to let go.
Stiff
Cool
You.

I'm so tired of running.
I'm dead, you know,
I died too.
A broken record, his voice, again and again,
bad, bad news is what he said.
Your father — broken and shattered and defeated too.

Holding the frozen hand,
I stood
begging someone to make this stop.
Stop.
Stop.

Like you,
your heart.
I remember that first time
pregnant
stethoscope to my belly
your heartbeat
full of promise
full of hope.
No more
my head on your chest
listening
listening
wondering where the people were who could make
    this stop...
and his voice
dull as distant thunder
unexpected lightning
stuns.
Stunned,
frozen in time
you and I.
Giving birth,
forceps —
did we force you into this world?
Yet, how quickly you disappeared.

I've got nothing
No hope
no reason
everything else fades.
I can't connect.
I'm behind the veil
thin, black.

I can't feel
hear.
Nothing.
My head pressed against your chest
waiting for the sound that will never, ever come.

Before It's Too Late

Before it's too late
I'm going to find my way to you.
I search in reckless dreams
and deadly nightmares
wondering if this is the way it will always be,
held
far from you
by life's twisted tentacles.
I'm screaming your name,
can you hear me?
Twenty-one years
have disappeared
vaporized
leaving me alone,
my soul shredded.
Punishing fate has played her cheating hand.
I can't go on

without relief.
My weeping blackens the clouds
and you
are somewhere
yet nowhere near.

Before it's too late
I want to find my way
through thorn-framed dreams
skin sliced, but I don't care.
What is there, without you here?
Your laugh,
your spirit.
"At least you have two others," they say
as they turn away.
They don't know that in losing a child
nothing can replace
that solitary place.

Before it's too late,
I've got to claw my way to you
wherever you may be
lost
deteriorating
or is that me?
Rotting
disappearing
trapped in a grave.

Before it's too late
I've got to find my way to you.
Razor blades are sweet distractions;
nothing takes the place of you.

This pain
leaves me stranded
on broken glass
I stand naked
hoping for the gash
that brings me to you.

Before it's too late,
I've got to find my way to you —
I break imaginary vases
and strip flowers bare.
I've nothing left
here
and nothing fills this aching heart.
Eyes burned open
streaks of death mute the day
leaving me hopeless.

Before it's too late
I'm going to build a ladder
climb a tree
tightrope walk on sharp sun rays —
balance once no problem for me.
I wonder if falling could ease this pain
or bring you closer to me?

Before it's too late
I'm going to find my way
crack the code
rip the veil
track you down.
Where have they taken you?
Why leave me behind

to follow footprints that
evaporate?

Before it's too late
I'm going to ride arrows
through death's chambers
slice her curtain
seduce her sentinels
and find my way to you.

Lost Self

Fate

Trees or shadows ahead?
Hard to know
these days
since death robbed my eyes
leaving a blurry dream
She's a siren really,
fate . . .
dressed in breezy gowns.
Her seductive melody
weaves
smoky
blue
notes
that I hear distinctly —
One merely follows the sounds
when death has stolen the light.

Rearview Mirror

Sometimes, at night, I scan the sky.
Always one star will call to me.
Once, we touched that high.
Do you remember?
Touching a star.
Fingers charred.
We didn't care.
Not then.

This morning's rain reminds me —
don't hold on to the glory of brief spring days
in this otherwise gloomy season.
Even as I watched a spring-struck meadowlark
disappear into the climbing sun,
I never really believed winter was over.
Life is not that simple.

And then,
your call.
I had to smile.
I'd wondered where your journey had taken you,
why you left no footprints —
especially with *this* winter's way of grasping
clutching everything
into its cold, empty arms.

Glad
to hear from you.
Wondering
why you disappeared,
reappeared.

A glance in a rearview mirror.
Nothing looks the same.
I do it anyway.
Spend a lot of time looking behind.
Watching for ghosts.
Hoping for just a moment,
death will give my son a break and let him sit next
   to me,
hold my hand,
just one kiss —
Surely you can understand
Sometimes, someone will pass me on the street
and for a moment I'll think it's him . . .

Driving through the streets.
Peering into rearview mirrors.
Wishing I could go back . . . God . . . so many years ago
and do everything over.

Right.
This time.
Eyes wide open instead of shifty and slanty and
  self-absorbed.

Driven.
Been driven for so long.
And tired.
Tired of the fight.
Tired of holding back all the pain
and guilt
and sorrow,
wishing I could somehow have one chance to be
  different,
to change the course . . .

If I could
reach to a star
slip my finger into the socket.
Electrocution...
designer drug
better than satin
better than silk
better than a stranger's touch
and desires never to be fulfilled.

Rearview mirrors.
Wishing for ghosts to materialize.
Watching strangers cross the street.
But there's only tragic
thin silhouettes.
A cruel mirage . . .
death's grim masquerade.

Valentine Date

I'm not going on a Valentine's date.
Ruby's too reckless
and I can't survive
her
at the wheel.
Too many times
we ended up
slow dancing on a country road,
or in a field of creamy flowers
or kissing in shadows
of dead-end streets.
A mistake
with her.

She gives me nickel-bags of lust for free,
one taste
I crave.

Wind whipping through my hair
daisy-chain bondage
starry-eyed romance,
we don't look back
through slippery-sloped infidelities.
Shoot passion
dirty needles
no regrets
those days
we committed heart felonies
and escaped
unscathed.

A Valentine's date
that shouldn't be
is trouble city
and so is she.

Ruby

She moves across the room in a lacy slip.
Suitcase by the door
silk sheets folded
glitter concealed in sachet bags.

At the foot of the bed,
her ruby shoes shimmer.
On the bureau, her velvet hat.
Red-veiled
she's mystery
and all magic that I could be.

In the shadows, I watch her dress.
"When the shoes are on, it's over,"
she whispers
in a quiet room.
It's just the beginning,

I try to say
but the words
coagulate.

She spills into a glittery dress,
gives me an oblique glance.
"One last chance."
Muddy
vision
hard to see
her slide a foot into the shoe.

Last-chance flash
she disappears,
nothing
but a faint red glow.

I crawl to the foot of the bed
cheek flush to the hardwood floor
still warm
where she used to be.

Searching for Clues

She's left withered petals along the way.
I follow uncertain,
mesmerized by the scent of her perfume,
gardenias and roses.
Far ahead, a dim light zigzags through the trees.
She's riding a firefly, at least it seems,
twirling and fluttering.
I'm depleted,
and far behind.

She's wearing the ruby shoes.
Once they glittered at the foot of my bed,
those days
when she let me slip them on . . .
I danced across a shooting star
left traces of lipstick on many beds

strangers now
even so . . .

Up ahead, the light disappears.
I start to run
desperate not to lose sight
of what I used to be.
There's something about glitter that leaves me
    breathless . . .

On my knees,
I search for the scent of gardenias and roses.
Petals like her skin
when lovers touched her;
when she was me
and I wore diamonds in my hair
and left silver dust wherever I walked.
I remember
dancing cheek to cheek with a shadowy dream
tangoing above lava seas
I was hot...
I *think* that was me.

I'm searching for clues —
the light flickers between the trees
golden sequins sewn to velvet.
She shows herself
she's teasing me,
that woman,
the temptress I used to be.

She's left clues everywhere
but I still can't see

where she's leading me.
I'm trying to catch her
harness her
jump into her and dance the night in ecstasy.
That's how it used to be
when I was her
and she was me.

Exorcised

I dig deep
looking for the talisman
missing since the day I lost
my soul,
Ruby, she called herself,
neon flame
knew how to burn
turn
darkness into gold.
Electric flamenco dancers
were lined in blue
and every heart she touched
trembled.
Pleasure
bound us all.

She was the scarlet meteor
streaking across the sky.
Everyone stepped outside
to see,
stayed out late
to anticipate
her
reckless style.
We traveled with rogues
flirted with hit men
didn't we . . .

But those groggy mornings after
when I was charred
seemingly scarred
I gazed in the mirror
and pleaded for mercy.

Holy water seared my breasts
incense burned
verbal charms
incantations
by every knowing therapist.
Playing by the rules
I carved her firestorm out of me.

She packed her bags
walked out, didn't look back,
disappeared
when the coast was clear.
I slammed into normal life.
Lava soon solidified;
volcanic glass

has no crystals.
We've driven out the demon
is what they said.

I dig for the talisman
stir eye-of-bat memories
into my caldron heart.
Spells to conjure neon flames,
voodoo dolls with gemstone names.
A faint sorcery
left in me?
I try to pull
the needle free.

Emptying the Hand

Tight-fisted once,
forced open,
streams of rhinestones
tumble to a glossy hardwood floor.

Glittery sparks in all directions.
One step,
careful not to slip,
floor so slick
and I've no traction.
Doesn't matter,
rhinestone path beckons me.
Once-locked fist
pried open.

Wonder if there's something more —
sound of rhinestones

spilling to the floor.
A vacant hardness in my chest
one step
not to slide
or glide.
Looking down on empty hands
blood-streaked fingers —
is that your name carved
in my arm?
In my heart?
It's hard to feel any more.

A blade's a blade —
it's all the same to me.
Blood-soaked
rhinestones roll across the floor.
I've lost touch with what I'm searching for.

Unsure
one step
empty hands
blood-stained palms
specks of scarlet bruise the floor
once so clean
now stained
disdain
in the mirror
shabbily dressed in yesterday's dreams
crimson puddle surrounds me.

One step
empty hands
slivers of hope needle me

but I'm no fool
no, not me.
An ocean of burgundy encircles me.
In the mirror
I can see
conquered eyes staring back at me.
Dreams about a dark-red sea,
all that warmth
overcoming me.

A stark room
with dead reflections.
Rhinestones echo as they scatter.
One step
emptying the hand
slow-motion diamonds,
false and cheap,
crash from bloody fingers
to a polished hardwood floor.

Footsteps

I remember
when momentary pleasures brought no regret.
Those days, before the need to check
over my shoulder,
everything I touched
snapped with blue sparks.

Now, I regard every step.
Not like it used to be,
when I sprinkled stars
upon my breasts
and hid fire in my locket.

Once . . .
I harnessed the night,
painted words in silver-moon ink
and there was nothing I couldn't try

122

just to see
if I could.
The world was mine.
Dressed in sequined shoes
and silky lies,
I was fatal enchantment
in crimson disguise.

But now hallucinations
run amok.
When I close my eyes I see
his slippery shadow
slither through dark trees.
He watches every step I take.
Never lets up —
footsteps echo like love's deceit —
this stalker's melody.

Eros with his poisoned barb,
Venus watches from afar.
In the darkness
through the trees
something's closing in on me.

Newly Blind

This is it,
all that's left —
a cruel desert stretched as far as I can see.
A swift breeze snaps
sand
stings
bare flesh numb.

Head bowed, I see
sunlight mirrored
harsh on my eyes
already singed from too many tears.
A tattered scarf protects my face
suffocating yesterday's sobs.

I'd collapse if someone could show me how
to give way to the fall.

I'd capsize, gratefully —
Dear God, can't you see?
I've forgotten how.

This is it —
all that's left.
Endless desert surrounds me.
A mistress breeze whips continually
as night slowly devours her fury.
Daylight melts to a thick black sea
studded with flickering memories...

When darkness was my lover,
we were desperados
she and I
heat felt good
and everything
crackled with hot, sweet life,
fire and ice . . .
Ah those nights!
But while slinky silk
drifted to the floor
the truth of fleeting romance was soon revealed.
I thought I'd never survive
lost love
back then . . .

Heart halves, as far as I can see,
are scattered like abandoned shells.
Death's pas de deux —
that clever dance
slick, sly,
smooth glissade

to this desert floor
where
unclaimed hearts lay hollow.
Skeletons
and nothing more.

Mirage wavering
in the sinking sun.
I'm staring at me
eyes burnt
soul pinched by hunger that once stung
now deteriorating into numb.

This is it —
all that's left.
Scorched sand cools as night does her dirty work.
Once, I believed sunrise meant **just another day** —
yesterday's finale,
bookmarked with tomorrow's hope.
I'd wake up, knowing, *I start here.*
Not realizing death had a message for me.
Those days were mere luxury.

The dark angel has danced with me
trapped me in her misery
brutal, her intensity.
I'm nothing now
but deadened.
Will I ever come home to me?
Fast-fading mirage — don't disappear.
I'm losing track of who I used to be.

Eyes burnt from too many tears

Twilight sleep
newly blind.
That's all that's left of me.

I'd collapse if someone could show me how
knees give way
fall to the ground.
Visionless
a soul that's stripped
reading sand-Braille words
with blistered fingertips.

Storm Season

Like this —
gazing out to the sea
moaning waves linger on too-smooth sand
Cold air laps the uninhabited sky —
no birds soar storm-season nights
like this
Love is a silhouette,
deceives even the thin light,
as she wanders
aimless
below the jackknifed moon.

Diamond Arrows

I walk down deserted streets
sometime after midnight.
Danger drips from grimy buildings,
and oozes in darkened alleys.
I keep moving —
with a glance from side to side.
A risky place, but I don't care.
I'm looking for Ruby.

I flash a wrinkled photograph
to whomever will give me time.
A drunk pilot said
he'd played craps with her;
said she was dressed to the nines.

A hat with the veil,
red-sequined shoes,
and pin on her low-cut dress.

"The pin was mine, I lost the game,"
he said with a devilish grin.
"Three diamond arrows and one gold bow."
That woman plays to win."

I stuff my hands into my pockets.
The familiar knot aches in my belly.
A new pin, she'd won?
It sickens me
to learn that she
is still gambling.

I hurry down a tangled maze
of side streets and dim alleys.
A flashlight is my only defense
against shifting shadows.
Windows are barred —
this side of town —
it's hard be certain why.
To keep life's perils from breaking in?
Or the pleasure of danger from escaping?

At the end of the alley, a neon sign flashes.
The name of the club is *Marco's*.
She was last seen here,
whispering in the ear
of a shady, low-voiced stranger.
A black fedora was tipped low on his brow —
"Obscured," they said of his face.

"But *her* — " and they smiled in a hungry way ...
"Her image was hard to erase."
Her eyes behind a netted veil,
seductive lips, slippery red —
She's hard to forget and is talked about
long after she's left.

The trail she leaves is lava-hot.
I'm on my way.
I'll find her.
Three diamond arrows
grace her breast.
She'd won them from a drunk pilot.

Faith

I used to feed on second chances:
cartwheeled over fault lines on callused hands.
Waterfall pain cascaded...
but I stayed dry
almost dozing,
unsuspecting.
Now —
armed, dark creatures
ride shadows through stained dreams.
Unkind life carves the flesh
and faith remains unseen.

Tourniquet

I'm wandering in a complex maze
of stray nights and lonesome days.
Memories hang like crooked portraits.
Back then, I could spin the pain with seductive
    smiles
and magical words.
Where is she — that woman I used to be?
Her spice and delights
and clever ways
dazzled and protected me.
I'm the walking dead
looking for her.

Heading down twisted passageways
in search of the goddess
to beg her release.

Pleasures rotting, dead on the vine
no markers, no map
nothing to guide me out of here.
I'm listening for an opening door
groping for a break in the walls
desperate to find my out.

I wish I smoked or drank —
anything —
I just need a fix that works.
Romance used to do the trick,
but now,
phantom pusher at my side talking about love's
    track marks
mainline love affairs
strangers with glittery eyes.
She offers me this and more.
"On the house." she says. "After all . . ."
Her whiskey voice is smooth.

She's peddling lust
but it won't work,
we both know that.
Can't get high, no matter what I do.
Even so,
no release
acidic life.
My back is flush against a concrete wall
as I slide to the slimy floor
and offer my arm to her, anyway.
Tourniquet once so sweet
now, too tight.
She whispers in my ear, "This is right."

A big lie:
Maybe this time.

This moment,
on the floor
soul knotted
teeth clenched
burn so bad
got to have
fire in my vein.

Morality Play

Sitting in the corner of a vacant room
my soul
still streaked from bloodbath days
I dream
hallucinate . . .
It's about strength now.
It's about fire
and hope
and day to day.
Morality play
right or wrong
good or bad.
I'm no longer willing to crumple.
It's about survival now —
Psyche waits patiently
as dusk spills
into tender night.

Eros tucks his wings,
lover or beast?
Hard to know
without the light
without the trust.
Deliver me
from penalty
my only sin
survival.

Eros slips into his dream.
Psyche soon begins her scheme,
sparks the lamp to steal a glance
ending her sweet, dark romance.

Interiors

Slouched in a doorway,
I opened my eyes
and realized I was conscious.
I tried to rise
as I held my heart,
knowing what love had cost me.

Eros stepped from the shadows
invited me to the sky.
He said he'd given up the juice
but still knew how to fly.
He'd come, he said, to lift the veil.
He knew my eyes were curtained.

I dropped the flashlight,
afraid the beam would cut him.
But he fearlessly pressed

the light to his outstretched jaw —
his face illuminating.

His arrows hung on a leafless branch.
His wings lay on the ground.
He said he'd learned
that soulless love
is
without redemption.

Venus had taught him a lesson —
locked him in a room
and made him confront
the love he'd defaced
until he was earnestly sober.

I cringed.
His words had hit a nerve.
He *knew* my soul was Ruby.
"She's the shell that draws the eye.
The pearl possesses value."
He looked sincere.
His eyes were clear.
Perhaps I'd take a ride . . .

Pearl

Beneath the fractured moon
now mending,
newly spun by industrious comets,
nighthawks dive.

I reach toward the sky
stretch
stretch
stretching
as far as I can —
to catch the tail of a plunging bird.

Dreamy light spirals from my fingers
in silver braids
swirling up.
Nighthawks dip

capture the shimmer
and lift it toward the sky.

I've molted,
escaped into
vaporous
make-believe me.
Tiara of stars in my hair
midnight draped over my shoulders.

Nighthawks swoop,
pull evening's curtain.
Cool
dark
make-believe me.
dancing a samba
across night's obsidian floor.

The moon's healing has begun.
A silver thread
weaves through fragmented light.
Nighthawks soar.
Dazzling,
make-believe me
follows close behind.

I step from the shackles
into someone new.
A radiant gem
pinned to the ebony sky
burning like a star,
bright
exotic

prism light . . .
daydreaming, light-streaming, make-believe me
dressed in moonbeams.

A grain of desert sand transforms
to lustrous
precious
pearl.
Sand gone wrong?
It's a matter of taste.
Pearl becomes me...
though I'm not the ruby I expected to be.

Disjointed moon
in slow repair
as nighthawks glide
and I
comb starlight
through my hair.

Fantasy

Last night I met Eros on a cloud.
Peering over the misty dream,
I saw fractured pieces of myself
reflecting harsh, blinding streaks of light,
pinned to the wall like a broken butterfly.
Eros has reminded me
to touch the sky.
Averted eyes,
silk ribbons in my hair,
we drifted in azure-blue make believe.

This morning, eyes opened,
I'm nailed to the wall.
Heart still leaks,
spirit shattered on the floor...
Between almost-closed blinds,

bright, strong swords of light
slash the room,
reminding me —
last night, I defied gravity.

Beach

Tiny shells beneath our feet,
soft sand
cool and yielding,
we're walking hand in hand.
The sky broken from too much rain
and the scent of spring
fresh
lures us
toward green-curved hills.
Sun pushes through —
that's fine,
I'm looking for some warmth . . .
Up ahead
orange poppies bow
and daisies dance in the slight breeze,
just enough
to lift my skirt —

that's okay,
I like to tease.
Sun flirts,
maybe?
Blue will push beyond the gray
this day
walking,
my hat swirls in the breeze.
I'm laughing,
and chasing after me
you follow.

Putty

See what you've done to me?
Hard shell persuaded into soft.
Sly seductions woven cleverly through imaginary
    bouquets,
fresh-cut fantasies of wildflowers fill a crystal vase
on the nightstand —
if I'd let myself believe.
You say you'd like to walk with me
as sunset storms the desert sky,
two shadows lengthening as the day fades.
You'd string colored lights
through the gloom —
that is, if I'd let myself believe.
Can't you see?
I want to be led —
hunger is good,
escape is better,

surely you'd agree?
Through a maze of twilight shadows
I'd be lost.
Thankfully,
in your palm
warm and pliant
I could be something more
— that is, if I believe.

Unstrung Heart

Throughout my soul's dark journey
the midnight bell has rung
I sit in an empty bed
heart unstrung.

Shattered spirit mouthing
a melody unsung
I climb from the sleepless bed
heart unstrung.

Desperate for the fire,
pendulum has swung.
I peer out the window
heart unstrung.

Dance with the shadow
across the serpent's tongue

step into the cool night
heart unstrung.

Eros aimed his bow
glimmering arrows flung
pierced through endless misery
to a heart unstrung.

Beneath a convalescing moon
in lazy circles spun,
I begin the slow rewind
of a heart unstrung.

LOOKING FOR NAIAD?

CHANGE OF HEART by Linda Hill. 176 pp. High fashion and love in a glamorous world.   ISBN 1-56280-238-0 $11.95

UNSTRUNG HEART by Robbi Sommers. 176 pp. Putting life in order again.   ISBN 1-56280-239-9   11.95

BIRDS OF A FEATHER by Jackie Calhoun. 240 pp. Life begins with love.   ISBN 1-56280-240-2   11.95

THE DRIVE by Trisha Todd. 176 pp. The star of *Claire of the Moon* tells all!   ISBN 1-56280-237-2   11.95

BOTH SIDES by Saxon Bennett. 240 pp. A community of women falling in and out of love.   ISBN 1-56280-236-4   11.95

WATERMARK by Karin Kallmaker. 256 pp. One burning question . . . how to lead her back to love?   ISBN 1-56280-235-6   11.95

THE OTHER WOMAN by Ann O'Leary. 240 pp. Her roguish way draws women like a magnet.   ISBN 1-56280-234-8   11.95

SILVER THREADS by Lyn Denison.208 pp. Finding her way back to love . . .   ISBN 1-56280-231-3   11.95

CHIMNEY ROCK BLUES by Janet McClellan. 224 pp. 4th Tru North mystery.   ISBN 1-56280-233-X   11.95

OMAHA'S BELL by Penny Hayes. 208 pp. Orphaned Keeley Delaney woos the lovely Prudence Morris.   ISBN 1-56280-232-1   11.95

SIXTH SENSE by Kate Calloway. 224 pp. 6th Cassidy James mystery.   ISBN 1-56280-228-3   11.95

DAWN OF THE DANCE by Marianne K. Martin. 224 pp. A dance with an old friend, nothing more . . . yeah!   ISBN 1-56280-229-1   11.95

WEDDING BELL BLUES by Julia Watts. 240 pp. Love, family, and a recipe for success.   ISBN 1-56280-230-5   11.95

THOSE WHO WAIT by Peggy J. Herring. 160 pp. Two sisters . . . in love with the same woman.   ISBN 1-56280-223-2   11.95

WHISPERS IN THE WIND by Frankie J. Jones. 192 pp. "If you don't want this," she whispered, "all you have to say is 'stop.'" ISBN 1-56280-226-7   11.95

WHEN SOME BODY DISAPPEARS by Therese Szymanski. 192 pp. 3rd Brett Higgins mystery.   ISBN 1-56280-227-5   11.95

THE WAY LIFE SHOULD BE by Diana Braund. 240 pp. Which one will teach her the true meaning of love?   ISBN 1-56280-221-6   11.95

UNTIL THE END by Kaye Davis. 256pp. 3rd Maris Middleton mystery.   ISBN 1-56280-222-4   11.95

FIFTH WHEEL by Kate Calloway. 224 pp. 5th Cassidy James mystery.   ISBN 1-56280-218-6   11.95

JUST YESTERDAY by Linda Hill. 176 pp. Reliving all the passion of yesterday.   ISBN 1-56280-219-4   11.95

THE TOUCH OF YOUR HAND edited by Barbara Grier and Christine Cassidy. 304 pp. Erotic love stories by Naiad Press authors.   ISBN 1-56280-220-8   14.95

WINDROW GARDEN by Janet McClellan. 192 pp. They discover a passion they never dreamed possible.   ISBN 1-56280-216-X   11.95

PAST DUE by Claire McNab. 224 pp. 10th Carol Ashton mystery.   ISBN 1-56280-217-8   11.95

CHRISTABEL by Laura Adams. 224 pp. Two captive hearts and the passion that will set them free.   ISBN 1-56280-214-3   11.95

PRIVATE PASSIONS by Laura DeHart Young. 192 pp. An unforgettable new portrait of lesbian love . . .   ISBN 1-56280-215-1   11.95

BAD MOON RISING by Barbara Johnson. 208 pp. 2nd Colleen Fitzgerald mystery.   ISBN 1-56280-211-9   11.95

RIVER QUAY by Janet McClellan. 208 pp. 3rd Tru North mystery.   ISBN 1-56280-212-7   11.95

ENDLESS LOVE by Lisa Shapiro. 272 pp. To believe, once again, that love can be forever.   ISBN 1-56280-213-5   11.95

FALLEN FROM GRACE by Pat Welch. 256 pp. 6th Helen Black mystery.   ISBN 1-56280-209-7   11.95

THE NAKED EYE by Catherine Ennis. 208 pp. Her lover in the camera's eye . . .   ISBN 1-56280-210-0   11.95

OVER THE LINE by Tracey Richardson. 176 pp. 2nd Stevie Houston mystery.   ISBN 1-56280-202-X   11.95

JULIA'S SONG by Ann O'Leary. 208 pp. Strangely disturbing . . . strangely exciting.   ISBN 1-56280-197-X   11.95

LOVE IN THE BALANCE by Marianne K. Martin. 256 pp. Weighing the costs of love . . .   ISBN 1-56280-199-6   11.95

PIECE OF MY HEART by Julia Watts. 208 pp. All the stuff that dreams are made of —   ISBN 1-56280-206-2   11.95

MAKING UP FOR LOST TIME by Karin Kallmaker. 240 pp.
Nobody does it better . . .   ISBN 1-56280-196-1   11.95

GOLD FEVER by Lyn Denison. 224 pp. By author of *Dream
Lover.*   ISBN 1-56280-201-1   11.95

WHEN THE DEAD SPEAK by Therese Szymanski. 224 pp. 2nd
Brett Higgins mystery.   ISBN 1-56280-198-8   11.95

FOURTH DOWN by Kate Calloway. 240 pp. 4th Cassidy James
mystery.   ISBN 1-56280-205-4   11.95

A MOMENT'S INDISCRETION by Peggy J. Herring. 176 pp.
There's a fine line between love and lust . . . ISBN 1-56280-194-5   11.95

CITY LIGHTS/COUNTRY CANDLES by Penny Hayes. 208 pp.
About the women she has known . . .   ISBN 1-56280-195-3   11.95

POSSESSIONS by Kaye Davis. 240 pp. 2nd Maris Middleton
mystery.   ISBN 1-56280-192-9   11.95

A QUESTION OF LOVE by Saxon Bennett. 208 pp. Every
woman is granted one great love.   ISBN 1-56280-205-4   11.95

RHYTHM TIDE by Frankie J. Jones. 160 pp. . . . to desire
passionately and be passionately desired.   ISBN 1-56280-189-9   11.95

PENN VALLEY PHOENIX by Janet McClellan. 208 pp. 2nd
Tru North Mystery.   ISBN 1-56280-200-3   11.95

BY RESERVATION ONLY by Jackie Calhoun. 240 pp. A
chance for true happiness.   ISBN 1-56280-191-0   11.95

OLD BLACK MAGIC by Jaye Maiman. 272 pp. 9th Robin
Miller mystery.   ISBN 1-56280-175-9   11.95

LEGACY OF LOVE by Marianne K. Martin. 240 pp. Women
will do anything for her . . .   ISBN 1-56280-184-8   11.95

LETTING GO by Ann O'Leary. 160 pp. Laura, at 39, in love
with 23-year-old Kate.   ISBN 1-56280-183-X   11.95

LADY BE GOOD edited by Barbara Grier and Christine Cassidy.
288 pp. Erotic stories by Naiad Press authors. ISBN 1-56280-180-5   14.95

CHAIN LETTER by Claire McNab. 288 pp. 9th Carol Ashton
mystery.   ISBN 1-56280-181-3   11.95

NIGHT VISION by Laura Adams. 256 pp. Erotic fantasy romance
by "famous" author.   ISBN 1-56280-182-1   11.95

SEA TO SHINING SEA by Lisa Shapiro. 256 pp. Unable to resist
the raging passion . . .   ISBN 1-56280-177-5   11.95

THIRD DEGREE by Kate Calloway. 224 pp. 3rd Cassidy James
mystery.   ISBN 1-56280-185-6   11.95

WHEN THE DANCING STOPS by Therese Szymanski. 272 pp.
1st Brett Higgins mystery.   ISBN 1-56280-186-4   11.95

PHASES OF THE MOON by Julia Watts. 192 pp. . . . . hungry
for everything life has to offer.   ISBN 1-56280-176-7   11.95

BABY IT'S COLD by Jaye Maiman. 256 pp. 5th Robin Miller
mystery.   ISBN 1-56280-156-2   10.95

CLASS REUNION by Linda Hill. 176 pp. The girl from her
past . . .   ISBN 1-56280-178-3   11.95

DREAM LOVER by Lyn Denison. 224 pp. A soft, sensuous,
romantic fantasy.   ISBN 1-56280-173-1   11.95

FORTY LOVE by Diana Simmonds. 288 pp. Joyous, heart-
warming romance.   ISBN 1-56280-171-6   11.95

IN THE MOOD by Robbi Sommers. 160 pp. The queen of
erotic tension!   ISBN 1-56280-172-4   11.95

SWIMMING CAT COVE by Lauren Douglas. 192 pp. 2nd
Allison O'Neil Mystery.   ISBN 1-56280-168-6   11.95

THE LOVING LESBIAN by Claire McNab and Sharon Gedan.
240 pp. Explore the experiences that make lesbian love unique.
                                      ISBN 1-56280-169-4   14.95

COURTED by Celia Cohen. 160 pp. Sparkling romantic
encounter.   ISBN 1-56280-166-X   11.95

SEASONS OF THE HEART by Jackie Calhoun. 240 pp. Romance
through the years.   ISBN 1-56280-167-8   11.95

K. C. BOMBER by Janet McClellan. 208 pp. 1st Tru North
mystery.   ISBN 1-56280-157-0   11.95

LAST RITES by Tracey Richardson. 192 pp. 1st Stevie Houston
mystery.   ISBN 1-56280-164-3   11.95

EMBRACE IN MOTION by Karin Kallmaker. 256 pp. A whirlwind
love affair.   ISBN 1-56280-165-1   11.95

HOT CHECK by Peggy J. Herring. 192 pp. Will workaholic Alice
fall for guitarist Ricky?   ISBN 1-56280-163-5   11.95

OLD TIES by Saxon Bennett. 176 pp. Can Cleo surrender to a
passionate new love?   ISBN 1-56280-159-7   11.95

LOVE ON THE LINE by Laura DeHart Young. 176 pp. Will Stef
win Kay's heart?   ISBN 1-56280-162-7   11.95

DEVIL'S LEG CROSSING by Kaye Davis. 192 pp. 1st Maris
Middleton mystery.   ISBN 1-56280-158-9   11.95

COSTA BRAVA by Marta Balletbo Coll. 144 pp. Read the book,
see the movie!   ISBN 1-56280-153-8   11.95

MEETING MAGDALENE & OTHER STORIES by
Marilyn Freeman. 144 pp. Read the book, see the movie!
                                      ISBN 1-56280-170-8   11.95

SECOND FIDDLE by Kate 208 pp. 2nd P.I. Cassidy James
mystery.   ISBN 1-56280-169-6   11.95

LAUREL by Isabel Miller. 128 pp. By the author of the beloved
Patience and Sarah.   ISBN 1-56280-146-5   10.95

LOVE OR MONEY by Jackie Calhoun. 240 pp. The romance of
real life.   ISBN 1-56280-147-3   10.95

SMOKE AND MIRRORS by Pat Welch. 224 pp. 5th Helen Black
Mystery.   ISBN 1-56280-143-0   10.95

DANCING IN THE DARK edited by Barbara Grier & Christine
Cassidy. 272 pp. Erotic love stories by Naiad Press authors.
                                              ISBN 1-56280-144-9   14.95

TIME AND TIME AGAIN by Catherine Ennis. 176 pp. Passionate
love affair.   ISBN 1-56280-145-7   10.95

PAXTON COURT by Diane Salvatore. 256 pp. Erotic and wickedly
funny contemporary tale about the business of learning to live
together.   ISBN 1-56280-114-7   10.95

INNER CIRCLE by Claire McNab. 208 pp. 8th Carol Ashton
Mystery.   ISBN 1-56280-135-X   11.95

LESBIAN SEX: AN ORAL HISTORY by Susan Johnson.
240 pp. Need we say more?   ISBN 1-56280-142-2   14.95

WILD THINGS by Karin Kallmaker. 240 pp. By the undisputed
mistress of lesbian romance.   ISBN 1-56280-139-2   11.95

THE GIRL NEXT DOOR by Mindy Kaplan. 208 pp. Just what
you d expect.   ISBN 1-56280-140-6   11.95

NOW AND THEN by Penny Hayes. 240 pp. Romance on the
westward journey.   ISBN 1-56280-121-X   11.95

HEART ON FIRE by Diana Simmonds. 176 pp. The romantic and
erotic rival of *Curious Wine*.   ISBN 1-56280-152-X   11.95

DEATH AT LAVENDER BAY by Lauren Wright Douglas. 208 pp.
1st Allison O'Neil Mystery.   ISBN 1-56280-085-X   11.95

YES I SAID YES I WILL by Judith McDaniel. 272 pp. Hot
romance by famous author.   ISBN 1-56280-138-4   11.95

FORBIDDEN FIRES by Margaret C. Anderson. Edited by Mathilda
Hills. 176 pp. Famous author's "unpublished" Lesbian romance.
                                              ISBN 1-56280-123-6   21.95

SIDE TRACKS by Teresa Stores. 160 pp. Gender-bending
Lesbians on the road.   ISBN 1-56280-122-8   10.95

WILDWOOD FLOWERS by Julia Watts. 208 pp. Hilarious and
heart-warming tale of true love.   ISBN 1-56280-127-9   10.95

NEVER SAY NEVER by Linda Hill. 224 pp. Rule #1: Never get
involved with . . .   ISBN 1-56280-126-0   11.95

THE WISH LIST by Saxon Bennett. 192 pp. Romance through
the years.   ISBN 1-56280-125-2   10.95

OUT OF THE NIGHT by Kris Bruyer. 192 pp. Spine-tingling
thriller.   ISBN 1-56280-120-1   10.95

LOVE'S HARVEST by Peggy J. Herring. 176 pp. by the author of
Once More With Feeling.   ISBN 1-56280-117-1   10.95

FAMILY SECRETS by Laura DeHart Young. 208 pp. Enthralling
romance and suspense.   ISBN 1-56280-119-8   10.95

INLAND PASSAGE by Jane Rule. 288 pp. Tales exploring conven-
tional & unconventional relationships.   ISBN 0-930044-56-8   10.95

DOUBLE BLUFF by Claire McNab. 208 pp. 7th Carol Ashton
Mystery.   ISBN 1-56280-096-5   10.95

BAR GIRLS by Lauran Hoffman. 176 pp. See the movie, read
the book!   ISBN 1-56280-115-5   10.95

THE FIRST TIME EVER edited by Barbara Grier & Christine
Cassidy. 272 pp. Love stories by Naiad Press authors.
                                              ISBN 1-56280-086-8   14.95

MISS PETTIBONE AND MISS McGRAW by Brenda Weathers.
208 pp. A charming ghostly love story.   ISBN 1-56280-151-1   10.95

CHANGES by Jackie Calhoun. 208 pp. Involved romance and
relationships.   ISBN 1-56280-083-3   10.95

FAIR PLAY by Rose Beecham. 256 pp. An Amanda Valentine
Mystery.   ISBN 1-56280-081-7   10.95

PAYBACK by Celia Cohen. 176 pp. A gripping thriller of romance,
revenge and betrayal.   ISBN 1-56280-084-1   10.95

THE BEACH AFFAIR by Barbara Johnson. 224 pp. Sizzling
summer romance/mystery/intrigue.   ISBN 1-56280-090-6   10.95

GETTING THERE by Robbi Sommers. 192 pp. Nobody does it
like Robbi!   ISBN 1-56280-099-X   10.95

FINAL CUT by Lisa Haddock. 208 pp. 2nd Carmen Ramirez
Mystery.   ISBN 1-56280-088-4   10.95

FLASHPOINT by Katherine V. Forrest. 256 pp. A Lesbian
blockbuster!   ISBN 1-56280-079-5   10.95

CLAIRE OF THE MOON by Nicole Conn. Audio Book —
Read by Marianne Hyatt.   ISBN 1-56280-113-9   16.95

FOR LOVE AND FOR LIFE: INTIMATE PORTRAITS OF
LESBIAN COUPLES by Susan Johnson. 224 pp.
                                              ISBN 1-56280-091-4   14.95

DEVOTION by Mindy Kaplan. 192 pp. See the movie — read
the book!   ISBN 1-56280-093-0   10.95

SOMEONE TO WATCH by Jaye Maiman. 272 pp. 4th Robin
Miller Mystery.   ISBN 1-56280-095-7   10.95

GREENER THAN GRASS by Jennifer Fulton. 208 pp. A young
woman — a stranger in her bed.   ISBN 1-56280-092-2   10.95

TRAVELS WITH DIANA HUNTER by Regine Sands. Erotic
lesbian romp. Audio Book (2 cassettes)   ISBN 1-56280-107-4   16.95

CABIN FEVER by Carol Schmidt. 256 pp. Sizzling suspense
and passion.   ISBN 1-56280-089-1   10.95

THERE WILL BE NO GOODBYES by Laura DeHart Young. 192
pp. Romantic love, strength, and friendship.   ISBN 1-56280-103-1   10.95

FAULTLINE by Sheila Ortiz Taylor. 144 pp. Joyous comic
lesbian novel.   ISBN 1-56280-108-2   9.95

OPEN HOUSE by Pat Welch. 176 pp. 4th Helen Black Mystery.
                                          ISBN 1-56280-102-3   10.95

ONCE MORE WITH FEELING by Peggy J. Herring. 240 pp.
Lighthearted, loving romantic adventure.   ISBN 1-56280-089-2   11.95

WHISPERS by Kris Bruyer. 176 pp. Romantic ghost story.
                                          ISBN 1-56280-082-5   10.95

NIGHT SONGS by Penny Mickelbury. 224 pp. 2nd Gianna
Maglione Mystery.   ISBN 1-56280-097-3   10.95

GETTING TO THE POINT by Teresa Stores. 256 pp. Classic
southern Lesbian novel.   ISBN 1-56280-100-7   10.95

PAINTED MOON by Karin Kallmaker. 224 pp. Delicious
Kallmaker romance.   ISBN 1-56280-075-2   11.95

THE MYSTERIOUS NAIAD edited by Katherine V. Forrest &
Barbara Grier. 320 pp. Love stories by Naiad Press authors.
                                          ISBN 1-56280-074-4   14.95

DAUGHTERS OF A CORAL DAWN by Katherine V. Forrest.
240 pp. Tenth Anniversay Edition.   ISBN 1-56280-104-X   11.95

BODY GUARD by Claire McNab. 208 pp. 6th Carol Ashton
Mystery.   ISBN 1-56280-073-6   11.95

CACTUS LOVE by Lee Lynch. 192 pp. Stories by the beloved
storyteller.   ISBN 1-56280-071-X   9.95

SECOND GUESS by Rose Beecham. 216 pp. An Amanda
Valentine Mystery.   ISBN 1-56280-069-8   9.95

A RAGE OF MAIDENS by Lauren Wright Douglas. 240 pp.
6th Caitlin Reece Mystery.   ISBN 1-56280-068-X   10.95

TRIPLE EXPOSURE by Jackie Calhoun. 224 pp. Romantic
drama involving many characters.   ISBN 1-56280-067-1   10.95

PERSONAL ADS by Robbi Sommers. 176 pp. Sizzling short
stories.   ISBN 1-56280-059-0   11.95

CROSSWORDS by Penny Sumner. 256 pp. 2nd Victoria Cross
Mystery.   ISBN 1-56280-064-7   9.95

SWEET CHERRY WINE by Carol Schmidt. 224 pp. A novel of
suspense.   ISBN 1-56280-063-9   9.95

CERTAIN SMILES by Dorothy Tell. 160 pp. Erotic short stories.
                                          ISBN 1-56280-066-3   9.95

EDITED OUT by Lisa Haddock. 224 pp. 1st Carmen Ramirez
Mystery.   ISBN 1-56280-077-9   9.95

SMOKEY O by Celia Cohen. 176 pp. Relationships on the
playing field.   ISBN 1-56280-057-4   9.95

KATHLEEN O'DONALD by Penny Hayes. 256 pp. Rose and
Kathleen find each other and employment in 1909 NYC.
                                           ISBN 1-56280-070-1   9.95

STAYING HOME by Elisabeth Nonas. 256 pp. Molly and Alix
want a baby . . . or do they?   ISBN 1-56280-076-0   10.95

TRUE LOVE by Jennifer Fulton. 240 pp. Six lesbians searching
for love in all the "right" places.   ISBN 1-56280-035-3   11.95

KEEPING SECRETS by Penny Mickelbury. 208 pp. 1st Gianna
Maglione Mystery.   ISBN 1-56280-052-3   9.95

THE ROMANTIC NAIAD edited by Katherine V. Forrest &
Barbara Grier. 336 pp. Love stories by Naiad Press authors.
                                           ISBN 1-56280-054-X   14.95

UNDER MY SKIN by Jaye Maiman. 336 pp. 3rd Robin Miller
Mystery.   ISBN 1-56280-049-3.   11.95

CAR POOL by Karin Kallmaker. 272pp. Lesbians on wheels
and then some!   ISBN 1-56280-048-5   11.95

NOT TELLING MOTHER: STORIES FROM A LIFE by Diane
Salvatore. 176 pp. Her 3rd novel.   ISBN 1-56280-044-2   9.95

GOBLIN MARKET by Lauren Wright Douglas. 240pp. 5th Caitlin
Reece Mystery.   ISBN 1-56280-047-7   10.95

FRIENDS AND LOVERS by Jackie Calhoun. 224 pp. Mid-
western Lesbian lives and loves.   ISBN 1-56280-041-8   11.95

BEHIND CLOSED DOORS by Robbi Sommers. 192 pp. Hot,
erotic short stories.   ISBN 1-56280-039-6   11.95

CLAIRE OF THE MOON by Nicole Conn. 192 pp. See the
movie — read the book!   ISBN 1-56280-038-8   11.95

SILENT HEART by Claire McNab. 192 pp. Exotic Lesbian
romance.   ISBN 1-56280-036-1   11.95

THE SPY IN QUESTION by Amanda Kyle Williams. 256 pp.
A Madison McGuire Mystery.   ISBN 1-56280-037-X   9.95

SAVING GRACE by Jennifer Fulton. 240 pp. Adventure and
romantic entanglement.   ISBN 1-56280-051-5   11.95

CURIOUS WINE by Katherine V. Forrest. 176 pp. Tenth Anniver-
sary Edition. The most popular contemporary Lesbian love story.
                                           ISBN 1-56280-053-1   11.95
        Audio Book (2 cassettes)   ISBN 1-56280-105-8   16.95

CHAUTAUQUA by Catherine Ennis. 192 pp. Exciting, romantic
adventure.   ISBN 1-56280-032-9   9.95

A PROPER BURIAL by Pat Welch. 192 pp. 3rd Helen Black
Mystery.   ISBN 1-56280-033-7   9.95

SILVERLAKE HEAT: A Novel of Suspense by Carol Schmidt.
240 pp. Rhonda is as hot as Laney's dreams.   ISBN 1-56280-031-0   9.95

LOVE, ZENA BETH by Diane Salvatore. 224 pp. The most talked
about lesbian novel of the nineties!   ISBN 1-56280-030-2   10.95

A DOORYARD FULL OF FLOWERS by Isabel Miller. 160 pp.
Stories incl. 2 sequels to *Patience and Sarah*.   ISBN 1-56280-029-9   9.95

MURDER BY TRADITION by Katherine V. Forrest. 288 pp. 4th
Kate Delafield Mystery.   ISBN 1-56280-002-7   11.95

THE EROTIC NAIAD edited by Katherine V. Forrest & Barbara
Grier. 224 pp. Love stories by Naiad Press authors.
                                            ISBN 1-56280-026-4   14.95

DEAD CERTAIN by Claire McNab. 224 pp. 5th Carol Ashton
Mystery.   ISBN 1-56280-027-2   9.95

CRAZY FOR LOVING by Jaye Maiman. 320 pp. 2nd Robin Miller
Mystery.   ISBN 1-56280-025-6   11.95

UNCERTAIN COMPANIONS by Robbi Sommers. 204 pp.
Steamy, erotic novel.   ISBN 1-56280-017-5   11.95

A TIGER'S HEART by Lauren W. Douglas. 240 pp. 4th Caitlin
Reece Mystery.   ISBN 1-56280-018-3   9.95

PAPERBACK ROMANCE by Karin Kallmaker. 256 pp. A
delicious romance.   ISBN 1-56280-019-1   10.95

THE LAVENDER HOUSE MURDER by Nikki Baker. 224 pp.
2nd Virginia Kelly Mystery.   ISBN 1-56280-012-4   9.95

PASSION BAY by Jennifer Fulton. 224 pp. Passionate romance,
virgin beaches, tropical skies.   ISBN 1-56280-028-0   10.95

STICKS AND STONES by Jackie Calhoun. 208 pp. Contemporary
lesbian lives and loves.   ISBN 1-56280-020-5   9.95
Audio Book (2 cassettes)   ISBN 1-56280-106-6   16.95

UNDER THE SOUTHERN CROSS by Claire McNab. 192 pp.
Romantic nights Down Under.   ISBN 1-56280-011-6   11.95

GRASSY FLATS by Penny Hayes. 256 pp. Lesbian romance in
the '30s.   ISBN 1-56280-010-8   9.95

THE END OF APRIL by Penny Sumner. 240 pp. 1st Victoria
Cross Mystery.   ISBN 1-56280-007-8   8.95

KISS AND TELL by Robbi Sommers. 192 pp. Scorching stories
by the author of *Pleasures*.   ISBN 1-56280-005-1   11.95

STILL WATERS by Pat Welch. 208 pp. 2nd Helen Black Mystery.
                                            ISBN 0-941483-97-5   9.95

TO LOVE AGAIN by Evelyn Kennedy. 208 pp. Wildly romantic
love story.   ISBN 0-941483-85-1   11.95

IN THE GAME by Nikki Baker. 192 pp. 1st Virginia Kelly
Mystery.   ISBN 1-56280-004-3   9.95

STRANDED by Camarin Grae. 320 pp. Entertaining, riveting
adventure.   ISBN 0-941483-99-1   9.95

THE DAUGHTERS OF ARTEMIS by Lauren Wright Douglas.
240 pp. 3rd Caitlin Reece Mystery.   ISBN 0-941483-95-9   9.95

CLEARWATER by Catherine Ennis. 176 pp. Romantic secrets
of a small Louisiana town.   ISBN 0-941483-65-7   8.95

THE HALLELUJAH MURDERS by Dorothy Tell. 176 pp. 2nd
Poppy Dillworth Mystery.   ISBN 0-941483-88-6   8.95

BENEDICTION by Diane Salvatore. 272 pp. Striking, contemporary romantic novel.   ISBN 0-941483-90-8   11.95

COP OUT by Claire McNab. 208 pp. 4th Carol Ashton Mystery.

                                             ISBN 0-941483-84-3   10.95

THE BEVERLY MALIBU by Katherine V. Forrest. 288 pp. 3rd
Kate Delafield Mystery.   ISBN 0-941483-48-7   11.95

THE PROVIDENCE FILE by Amanda Kyle Williams. 256 pp.
A Madison McGuire Mystery.   ISBN 0-941483-92-4   8.95

I LEFT MY HEART by Jaye Maiman. 320 pp. 1st Robin Miller
Mystery.   ISBN 0-941483-72-X   11.95

THE PRICE OF SALT by Patricia Highsmith (writing as Claire
Morgan). 288 pp. Classic lesbian novel, first issued in 1952 . . .
acknowledged by its author under her own, very famous, name.
                                             ISBN 1-56280-003-5   11.95

SIDE BY SIDE by Isabel Miller. 256 pp. From beloved author of
Patience and Sarah.   ISBN 0-941483-77-0   10.95

STAYING POWER: LONG TERM LESBIAN COUPLES by
Susan E. Johnson. 352 pp. Joys of coupledom. ISBN 0-941-483-75-4   14.95

SLICK by Camarin Grae. 304 pp. Exotic, erotic adventure.
                                             ISBN 0-941483-74-6   9.95

NINTH LIFE by Lauren Wright Douglas. 256 pp. 2nd Caitlin
Reece Mystery.   ISBN 0-941483-50-9   9.95

PLAYERS by Robbi Sommers. 192 pp. Sizzling, erotic novel.
                                             ISBN 0-941483-73-8   9.95

MURDER AT RED ROOK RANCH by Dorothy Tell. 224 pp.
1st Poppy Dillworth Mystery.   ISBN 0-941483-80-0   8.95

A ROOM FULL OF WOMEN by Elisabeth Nonas. 256 pp.
Contemporary Lesbian lives.   ISBN 0-941483-69-X   9.95

THEME FOR DIVERSE INSTRUMENTS by Jane Rule. 208 pp.
Powerful romantic lesbian stories.   ISBN 0-941483-63-0   8.95

CLUB 12 by Amanda Kyle Williams. 288 pp. Espionage thriller
featuring a lesbian agent!   ISBN 0-941483-64-9   9.95

DEATH DOWN UNDER by Claire McNab. 240 pp. 3rd Carol
Ashton Mystery.   ISBN 0-941483-39-8   11.95

MONTANA FEATHERS by Penny Hayes. 256 pp. Vivian and
Elizabeth find love in frontier Montana.   ISBN 0-941483-61-4   9.95

THERE'S SOMETHING I'VE BEEN MEANING TO TELL YOU
Ed. by Loralee MacPike. 288 pp. Gay men and lesbians coming out
to their children.   ISBN 0-941483-44-4   9.95

LIFTING BELLY by Gertrude Stein. Ed. by Rebecca Mark. 104 pp.
Erotic poetry.   ISBN 0-941483-51-7   10.95

AFTER THE FIRE by Jane Rule. 256 pp. Warm, human novel by
this incomparable author.   ISBN 0-941483-45-2   8.95

PLEASURES by Robbi Sommers. 204 pp. Unprecedented
eroticism.   ISBN 0-941483-49-5   11.95

EDGEWISE by Camarin Grae. 372 pp. Spellbinding
adventure.   ISBN 0-941483-19-3   9.95

FATAL REUNION by Claire McNab. 224 pp. 2nd Carol Ashton
Mystery.   ISBN 0-941483-40-1   11.95

IN EVERY PORT by Karin Kallmaker. 228 pp. Jessica's sexy,
adventuresome travels.   ISBN 0-941483-37-7   11.95

OF LOVE AND GLORY by Evelyn Kennedy. 192 pp. Exciting
WWII romance.   ISBN 0-941483-32-0   10.95

CLICKING STONES by Nancy Tyler Glenn. 288 pp. Love
transcending time.   ISBN 0-941483-31-2   9.95

SOUTH OF THE LINE by Catherine Ennis. 216 pp. Civil War
adventure.   ISBN 0-941483-29-0   8.95

WOMAN PLUS WOMAN by Dolores Klaich. 300 pp. Supurb
Lesbian overview.   ISBN 0-941483-28-2   9.95

THE FINER GRAIN by Denise Ohio. 216 pp. Brilliant young
college lesbian novel.   ISBN 0-941483-11-8   8.95

LESSONS IN MURDER by Claire McNab. 216 pp. 1st Carol Ashton
Mystery.   ISBN 0-941483-14-2   11.95

YELLOWTHROAT by Penny Hayes. 240 pp. Margarita, bandit,
kidnaps Julia.   ISBN 0-941483-10-X   8.95

SAPPHISTRY: THE BOOK OF LESBIAN SEXUALITY by
Pat Califia. 3d edition, revised. 208 pp. ISBN 0-941483-24-X   12.95

CHERISHED LOVE by Evelyn Kennedy. 192 pp. Erotic Lesbian
love story.   ISBN 0-941483-08-8   11.95

THE SECRET IN THE BIRD by Camarin Grae. 312 pp. Striking,
psychological suspense novel.   ISBN 0-941483-05-3   8.95

TO THE LIGHTNING by Catherine Ennis. 208 pp. Romantic
Lesbian `Robinson Crusoe adventure.   ISBN 0-941483-06-1   8.95

DREAMS AND SWORDS by Katherine V. Forrest. 192 pp.
Romantic, erotic, imaginative stories.   ISBN 0-941483-03-7   11.95

MEMORY BOARD by Jane Rule. 336 pp. Memorable novel
about an aging Lesbian couple.   ISBN 0-941483-02-9   12.95

THE ALWAYS ANONYMOUS BEAST by Lauren Wright Douglas.
224 pp. 1st Caitlin Reece Mystery.   ISBN 0-941483-04-5   8.95

MURDER AT THE NIGHTWOOD BAR by Katherine V. Forrest.
240 pp. 2nd Kate Delafield Mystery.   ISBN 0-930044-92-4   11.95

WINGED DANCER by Camarin Grae. 228 pp. Erotic Lesbian
adventure story.   ISBN 0-930044-88-6   8.95

PAZ by Camarin Grae. 336 pp. Romantic Lesbian adventurer
with the power to change the world.   ISBN 0-930044-89-4   8.95

SOUL SNATCHER by Camarin Grae. 224 pp. A puzzle, an
adventure, a mystery — Lesbian romance.   ISBN 0-930044-90-8   8.95

THE LOVE OF GOOD WOMEN by Isabel Miller. 224 pp.
Long-awaited new novel by the author of the beloved *Patience
and Sarah*.   ISBN 0-930044-81-9   8.95

THE LONG TRAIL by Penny Hayes. 248 pp. Vivid adventures
of two women in love in the old west.   ISBN 0-930044-76-2   8.95

AN EMERGENCE OF GREEN by Katherine V. Forrest. 288
pp. Powerful novel of sexual discovery.   ISBN 0-930044-69-X   11.95

DESERT OF THE HEART by Jane Rule. 224 pp. A classic;
basis for the movie *Desert Hearts*.   ISBN 0-930044-73-8   11.95

SEX VARIANT WOMEN IN LITERATURE by Jeannette
Howard Foster. 448 pp. Literary history.   ISBN 0-930044-65-7   8.95

A HOT-EYED MODERATE by Jane Rule. 252 pp. Hard-hitting
essays on gay life; writing; art.   ISBN 0-930044-57-6   7.95

AMATEUR CITY by Katherine V. Forrest. 224 pp. 1st Kate
Delafield Mystery.   ISBN 0-930044-55-X   10.95

THE SOPHIE HOROWITZ STORY by Sarah Schulman. 176 pp.
Engaging novel of madcap intrigue.   ISBN 0-930044-54-1   7.95

THE YOUNG IN ONE ANOTHER'S ARMS by Jane Rule.
224 pp. Classic Jane Rule.   ISBN 0-930044-53-3   9.95

AGAINST THE SEASON by Jane Rule. 224 pp. Luminous,
complex novel of interrelationships.   ISBN 0-930044-48-7   8.95

These are just a few of the many Naiad Press titles — we are the oldest and
largest lesbian/feminist publishing company in the world. We also offer an
enormous selection of lesbian video products. Please request a complete
catalog. We offer personal service; we encourage and welcome direct mail
orders from individuals who have limited access to bookstores carrying our
publications.

LOOKING FOR NAIAD?